CLASSROOM CRITTERS

PLANS GONE WRONG

by Molly Beth Griffin

illustrated by Colin Jack

CONTENTS

CLASSROOM CRITTERS

**These five friends live within the walls,
nooks and crannies of a primary school.
They learn alongside the children every day,
even though the children don't see them!**

STELLA

Stella is a mouse. She loves her friends. She also loves children and school! She came into the school on a cold winter's day. She knew it would be her home forever. Her favourite subjects are history and music. She is always eager for a new day to start.

BO

Bo is a parakeet. He is a classroom pet. The friends let him out of his cage so they can play together. Bo loves to read. He goes home with his teacher at the weekend, but he always comes back to school to see his friends.

DELILAH

Delilah is a spider. She has always lived in the corners of the school. She is so small the children never notice her, but she is very clever. Delilah loves maths and computers and hates the broom!

NICO

Nico is a toad. He used to be a classroom pet. A child forgot to put him back into his tank one day. Now he lives with his friends. The whole school is his home! He can be grumpy, but he loves science and art. As Nico doesn't have fingers, he paints with his toes!

GOLDIE

Goldie is a goldfish. She is very wise. The friends ask her questions when they have a big decision to make. She gives good advice and lives in the library.

BIG PLANS

Stella the Mouse squeaked and sniffed. Her tummy rumbled. She found some bread crust and nibbled it. Stella shared her snack with Bo the Parakeet.

A fly buzzed around Stella. Nico the Toad snapped out his tongue and gobbled it up.

"I'll get the next one," said Delilah the Spider.

Just then the final bell rang. The children ran past the animal friends. They burst out of the school doors and into the sunny afternoon.

Stella, Nico, Delilah and Bo stayed out of the way. It was dangerous to get in the way of the children at the end of the day.

"Goodbye, children," Stella called. "Have fun. I will miss you!"

Stella didn't understand why the kids were so excited to go home. She was always sad after they left. She loved being at school!

Thankfully her friends knew how to cheer her up.

"Let's do something nice for the children," said Nico.

"Something special," said Delilah.

"That's a great idea! What shall we do?" Stella asked.

"I have the perfect plan," said Bo.

They spent that night plotting and planning.

Chapter 2

MUSIC AND PAINTING

The next morning, Stella didn't watch the children come in as usual.

She crept into the office. She scurried past the school secretary. She climbed up on top of the head's desk.

When the little red light turned on, she sang her best song into the microphone. Stella was a star! She loved singing to the kids.

But the head did NOT like mouse
music. She chased Stella right out
of the room!

"That did not go very well,"
Stella said.

"It's okay, Stella," said Nico. "The head is in charge of making the school run smoothly. I guess that means boring announcements."

Next Nico hopped to the art cupboard and found three colours of paint to mix. He dipped his toes into the mixture.

Nico began to paint the children a beautiful mural on the wall.

But the caretaker did NOT like toad paintings. He tried to catch Nico! Then he washed away all the paint.

"That did not go very well,"
Nico said.

"It's okay, Nico," said Delilah.
"The caretaker is in charge of
keeping the school clean. I guess
that means no paint on the walls."

Delilah crept into the canteen.
She spun amazing webs all over
the place. But the kitchen staff
quickly cleaned away her work.

"That did not go very well,"
Delilah said.

"It's okay, Delilah," Bo said.
"They have to make sure the food
is healthy. That means no spider
webs in the soup."

Then Bo flew into the nurse's office and got to work. He plucked and pecked.

But the school nurse shooed Bo out of there. She took one look at Bo's shredded tissue nests and threw them all away. Then she got out a new box of tissues.

"That did not go very well," Bo said.

"It's okay, Bo," said Stella. "The nurse has to look after kids who get ill at school. The nurse needs lots of fresh tissues. She probably needs a tidy office too."

"None of our plans worked," said Bo. "Now the school day is ending."

"I guess we can't do anything for the children," Stella sniffed.

Then she had one last idea. Goldie!

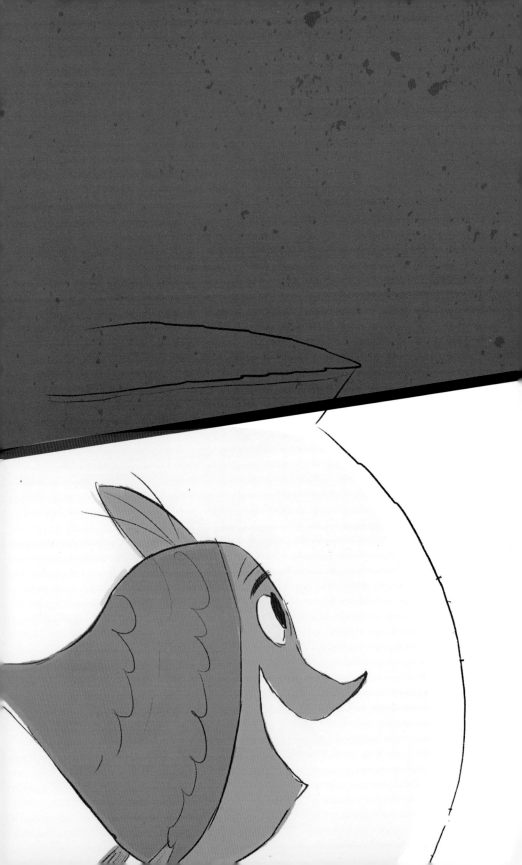

Chapter 3

SECRET GIFTS

The friends rushed to Goldie's bowl in the library. It was what they did whenever they had a question. They could always count on Goldie for help.

"Can we do anything special for the children?" Stella asked.

Goldie swam in a circle. Then she said, "Blub."

"One blub means yes!" said Nico. At least, that's what they thought it meant.

"What can we do, Goldie?" asked Delilah.

Goldie just stared at them.

"Maybe you mean . . . that we do things for the children already?" said Bo.

"Blub," said Goldie.

"Of course!" said Stella. "Bo and I clean up the children's scraps. And Nico and Delilah catch every fly and midges. Flies are annoying! Midges bite!"

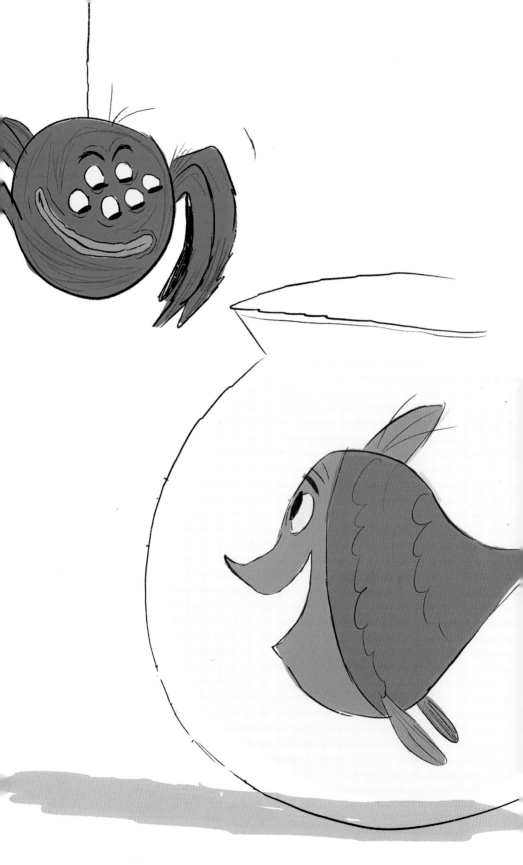

"True! The children really do need us," said Nico.

"Even if they don't know it," said Delilah.

"Maybe the best gifts are the secret ones," said Bo.

"Exactly! I feel so much better. Thanks, Goldie," Stella said.

Stella and her friends were tired after their big day. Even though their first plan didn't work, they were happy.

They knew that everybody in the school had an important job to do. Even them!

TALK ABOUT IT

1. If you had to pick one job at the school, what would it be? Why?

2. Talk about a time when you did something special for a friend, parent or teacher.

3. The animal friends go to Goldie for advice. Who do you go to for advice? Why?

WRITE ABOUT IT

1. Pretend you are throwing a surprise party for a friend. Make a list of supplies and a menu. Make sure you pick a fun theme!

2. Pick your favourite animal in the story and write a paragraph about things you have in common.

3. Write a blog post or newspaper article about the mysterious things happening around the school in this story.

MOLLY BETH GRIFFIN

Molly Beth Griffin is a writing teacher at the Loft Literary Center in Minneapolis, Minnesota, USA. She has written numerous picture books (including *Loon Baby* and *Rhoda's Rock Hunt*) and a YA novel (*Silhouette of a Sparrow*). Molly loves reading and hiking in all kinds of weather. She lives in South Minneapolis with her partner and two children.

COLIN JACK

Colin Jack has illustrated several books for children, including *Little Miss Muffet* (Flip-Side Rhymes), *Jack and Jill* (Flip-Side Rhymes), *Dragons from Mars*, *7 Days of Awesome* and *If You Happen to Have a Dinosaur*. He also works as a story artist and character designer at DreamWorks Studios. Colin splits his time living in California, USA, and Canada with his wife and two children.

PLENTY OF CRITTERY FUN!

Discover more at
www.raintree.co.uk

Raintree is an imprint of Capstone Global Library Limited, a company
incorporated in England and Wales having its registered office at 264
Banbury Road, Oxford, OX2 7DY – Registered company number: 6695582

www.raintree.co.uk
myorders@raintree.co.uk

Illustrated by Colin Jack
Designed by Ted Williams
Shutterstock: AVA Bitter, design element throughout,
Oleksandr Rybitskiy, design element throughout

Original illustrations © Capstone Global Library Limited 2020
Originated by Capstone Global Library Ltd
Printed and bound in India

ISBN 978 1 4747 7178 8

British Library Cataloguing in Publication Data:
A full catalogue record for this book is available from the British Library.